Arty *the* Artist

Arty *the* Artist

Leo Zarko

Illustrated by Patti Parish

God Bless

Arty was a wonderful young boy with a great smile. He was a wee bit on the short side with a cute little round belly and rosy red cheeks. Arty had a creative imagination and a love for art. He admired the great artists from the past and wanted to learn as much about them as he could.

Arty spent most of his time reading with his trusty cat da Vinci by his side. There were always plenty of art books lying around in his bedroom. Lucky for Arty, his parents supported his dream to become an artist. They bought him all the art books, supplies, and paints he needed.

Because he spent most of his time painting, Arty became quite good. When he didn't have a brush in his hand he was sketching with a pencil. His grades in school were fine, but Arty always counted on getting an A+ in art class.

As he read more about artists, Arty began to pick out his favorites. Something about the colors they used and their individual styles made him curious.

Arty decided to pick one artist per week and do his best to imitate them. He even wanted to start dressing up like them to make it as real as possible. His mom thought he was taking things a bit too far, but she went along with his idea because she loved him very much.

Arty wasted no time handing over a list of artists to his mom. She simply smiled and agreed to make the costumes he needed for inspiration.

Arty was surprised when his mom handed over his first costume so fast. Leonardo da Vinci would start him off. This of course made Arty very happy since he had named his cat after the famed artist.

Arty liked da Vinci's painting, *The Mona Lisa*, which might be the most famous painting of all time. Arty learned that Leonardo was born in Italy on April 15, 1452, which is known as "the Renaissance period." Even though Leonardo remains very famous, there are very few of his paintings in existence today.

Not only was Leonardo a great painter and sculptor, but he was also skilled in science, engineering, music, and the study of human anatomy. He was known as a gifted inventor and many of Leonardo's ideas can be seen in his sketching journals.

Arty decided that, like Leonardo, he would need a model to sit for him. Arty couldn't believe his luck because there was a girl named Mona in his class and she gladly said yes to becoming the new modern-day Mona Lisa—even though she had blond hair.

Arty was barely done with his first painting when his mom laid out a Claude Monet costume on his bed. Painting like Monet was going to be a real challenge. Mixing all those colors to match Claude's landscapes would be a lesson for sure. Arty had read about how Claude's new approach to art would change the look of how art was being created at that time. Claude, who was born November 14, 1840, also had other artist friends doing the same. This time period was known as

"Impressionism." Claude's mind was set on learning how light at different times of day could be used and how it affected the colors.

Monet painted beautiful pieces of art and many were of landscapes, gardens, ponds, and water lilies. When Claude was older he bought a large piece of land and designed it to fit his vision. Some of his most famous works came from his own yard.

Arty also read that Claude's mom wanted him to be an artist. This was something they both had in common. Arty asked his mom later that day if she would be his model. She simply said, "Yes, my wonderful son." Arty chose to recreate the painting called *Woman in a Garden* because it's so peaceful.

Arty was now into his third week of painting. This time he picked a female artist by the name of Mary

Cassatt who was born on May 22, 1844. She was born in Pennsylvania but admired many famous artists from Europe.

Her parents were not happy about her choice to become an artist, and at the time there were very few women in that career. As a young woman Mary decided that France was the place to be.

Male painters were successful and Mary wanted to be the same. When she first moved, Mary hadn't found her style just yet. She was allowed to visit museums and paint copies of the famous masterpieces. Soon she became good friends with the artists living there.

Mary worked hard but her success didn't happen right away. She almost quit art altogether in disappointment. In the art world, sometimes it takes awhile to get recognized. Mary pushed on and is now considered one of the true masters of art and a pioneering woman.

Arty chose to remake her painting called *Child in Straw Hat*. He asked his cousin Annabel to pose for this painting. He knew that Mary had chosen her relatives and friends to be models in her work. Annabel was also a good painter who admired Mary's work too.

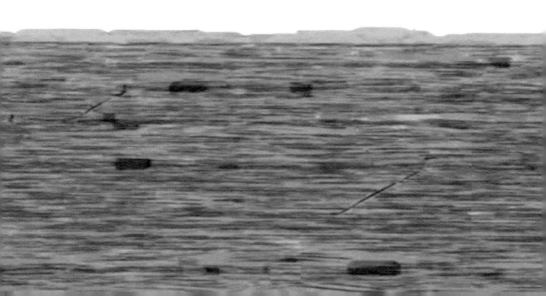

Arty moved on to the next artist, and perhaps one of the best-known artists in history, Vincent van Gogh. This time Arty really didn't know how to capture the style or look. The colors and paint used by van Gogh seemed thick and heavy, but appeared light and easy. Arty studied up on Vincent who was born on March 30, 1853. He was Dutch and created thousands of pieces of art. Like other artists of his time, van Gogh wanted a style that was all his own. Landscapes, still life, portraits, flowers and wheat fields were a big part of his work. Arty learned that painting a lot is probably the most important way to develop your own style.

Vincent didn't have an easy life and was sick often. Vincent had a brother named Theo who helped him with many things, including selling his work. Vincent wrote his brother many letters and now those letters help us discover what his life was like back then. There is a Vincent van Gogh museum in the Netherlands where people from all over the world can visit his works.

To honor van Gogh, Arty picked the painting, *The Sower*, and asked his older brother Eddie to model in this one.

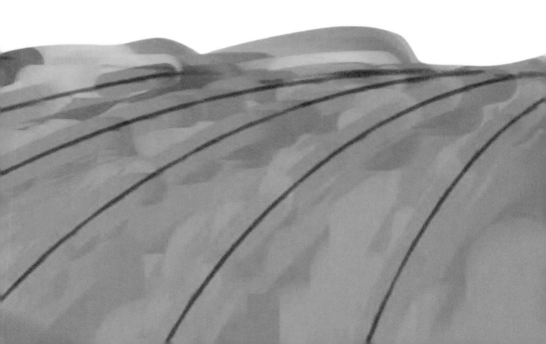

One weekend, Arty's mom decided her son needed a little time away from his brushes. She asked if he would like to go shopping with her. He stubbornly told her, "No, Mom. I have art to create."

She replied, "But I have a surprise if you come along."

Arty was unable to refuse a surprise, but he grabbed a sharpened pencil and a sketch book to bring with just in case. It was a warm day and Arty noticed his mom had a picnic basket in her hand. They stopped at a nice department store only to pick out a hat for her and one for him.

Next was a drive to a beautiful wheat field in the country where they stopped and picnicked. They talked very little as they ate lunch. Arty thought about the history of the artists he admired as he pulled out his sketch book and started drawing his mother in her lovely new hat with her long hair blowing around her face in the wind.

The day was growing long and Arty was curious about the surprise. As they drove home, his mother looked over and told him they had one more stop. Arty was hoping to get home and back to painting, but the surprise was right in front of him as they pulled into the parking lot of the art museum. All Arty could do was smile from ear to ear.

The following day, Arty was inspired and ready to get back to work on his next artist, Georges Seurat, who was born December 2, 1859.

Arty thought about the artists he chose and how it seemed they all changed art and the way people viewed it. Seurat was perhaps the start of a scientific awakening. He decided to let the viewer's eyes mix the colors in their minds rather than actually mixing the colors on canvas. This approach was called "pointillism." Arty had to look that word up. This new style had a lot to do with dots and lots of them. The closer you get to the work the more you see them, but by stepping back the painting becomes very clear.

Seurat was masterful with light and dark, warm and cold, lines and direction. It was mood setting as the art also had emotion and harmony. Seurat found art and music to be very similar. His most famous painting is called *A Afternoon on the Island of Lagrande Jette.*

Arty decided he would paint Seurat's *The Gardener* because he wanted his grandpa to model. Arty's grandpa agreed, but insisted they take a break for ice cream before finishing.

Arty was doing his best to paint as close as he could to the original work of each artist he admired. The next artist, Wassily Kandinski, who was born on December 16, 1866 in Russia, would teach Arty that anything is possible with art. Wassily viewed art in a spiritual way. He felt there was music in the colors and each color was its own note.

Wassily was a very smart man who studied law and economics along with art. Wassily was influenced by people who thought in new ways. He was fascinated with both color and form. He believed that the color was just as important as the object being painted. Later, as his style of work evolved, it was given a name known as "abstract art." Using circles, angles, shapes, and straight and curved lines, he created many masterpieces. Apart from being an artist he also became an author.

Arty was really happy about discovering this amazing artist. This new approach gave Arty the freedom to explore a new style without boundaries. This time there would be no model so Arty picked the painting called *Circles in a Circle*. Arty had no idea why Wassily's work touched him so much, but it certainly did.

Arty's mom kept up with his fast-moving painting projects. The next artist pushed Arty in a new direction once again. His name was Pablo Picasso, and he was born in Spain on October 25, 1881. Picasso's father was an artist and teacher of art. At an early age, Pablo was instructed in art by his father. It wasn't long before Pablo would be painting like some of the great artists before him.

Pablo was at the forefront of "modern art." He was known for periods or styles of art that where given names because of how they appeared. The "blue period" was because most of the work was in blue tones. The "rose period" was noted for shades of red, orange, and pink. The "cubism period" was a lot of square shapes. Picasso dated his paintings to keep track of how he created over time. Pablo not only painted but he also involved himself in other forms of art. He created thousands of pieces of art and became very famous.

For his Picasso project, Arty picked the painting called *The Old Guitarist*. Pete, a tall and slim friend of Arty's who happened to play guitar, was more than happy to pose. When Arty took breaks from painting, Pete would play a song. It was a kind of sharing of the arts.

Edward Hopper, who was born on July 22, 1882 in New York State, was to be Arty's next artist to explore. Hopper was a student of art and design. Most of his work was considered "realist art." He worked as an illustrator for magazines early on in order to make money, but that wasn't his interest. Edward used different styles of art like watercolor, pen and pencil, etching, and oils, and he was good at them all.

His paintings showed models in real life places. He used gas stations, railroads, hotels, and restaurants as his settings. He also painted landscapes, lighthouses, and seascapes.

Edward's work was something Arty enjoyed and admired. Arty decided to paint *Girl at Sewing Machine* because it reminded him of his mom. And, of course, all he had to do was watch her hard at work making his great looking costumes.

One day after school, Arty decided rather than go home and paint he'd take a long walk instead. There was a nature trail along the river that he liked to visit from time to time. Each time he looked at a tree, a field, or a wild creature he would ask himself, how would the great masters of art paint this? It seemed all this art stuff was making him overthink things.

Arty was studying because he wanted to be a good artist, but he knew in the end it was all about gathering inspiration. Like the artists before him, Arty needed to break new ground and develop his own style. He tried to imagine blue skies, landscapes, rivers, birds, and everything else in something far different from how others in the past viewed it.

As he walked along the river he let all his thoughts go and decided to let nature be his teacher. He discovered a nice freedom about this idea.

Another artist Arty really liked was Grant Wood, who was born in Iowa on February 13, 1891. Wood, along with other Midwest artists, changed the face of art once again with a new style. This style was known as "Regionalism," which means country or rural area.

Grant worked in a metal shop while in high school and after his graduation he attended art school. Wood also traveled to Europe to study the great art works of the masters. He later taught art at The University of Iowa School of Art for many years. His skills were many and not limited to just painting. He also worked in metal, wood, ceramics and other materials. One of the most famous paintings in the world was painted by Grant. It's called American Gothic. Arty decided that would be the painting he would use.

Arty couldn't wait to ask his dad and his dad's sister, Aunt Sonia, to pose. Arty's dad borrowed a pitchfork and some farmer clothes while his Aunt Sonia put together her outfit with the help of Arty's mom.

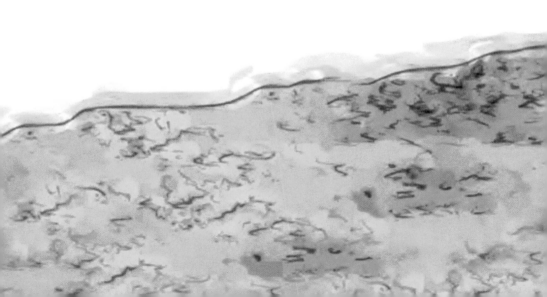

The last artist would be Norman Rockwell. Norman was considered more of an illustrator than an artist and didn't mind that title. Born February 3, 1894, Rockwell had a long-standing career with The Saturday Evening Post, a magazine he illustrated over 320 front covers for. Most of his work is considered to be a portrayal of American life.

The Boy Scouts of America kept Norman busy for over 60 years as he produced over 470 illustrations for them. Later in his life he would work for Look magazine as well. Rockwell even painted portraits of American presidents. It's said that he produced over 4,000 pieces of artwork over his career. He also added illustrations to a number of books. Rockwell's work is a look at America over a great many years.

There were endless pieces of Norman's art to pick from, but Arty thought that since he had to be in school all day, why not paint *Teacher's Birthday*? Arty's teacher was thrilled with the idea and let Arty sit in the back of the classroom with all his painting equipment.

Most artists are excited when doing what they do. It's during the creation of the work that something special is brought out.

Arty was both happy and a bit sad when his art project ended. His cat da Vinci, however, was glad because now he would be getting more attention.

Arty's parents asked him where he would be storing all his paintings. Arty replied, "Probably in my closet or under my bed."

Upon hearing his answer they both looked at each other with surprise. The day slowly passed and it was soon time for bed. The TV set was turned off and his parents gave the usual kiss and hug to Arty and his brother before tucking them in.

Arty's bedroom door wasn't closed all the way, allowing him to overhear his parents talk about having an art show for him over the upcoming weekend. Arty was supposed to be sleeping, so he didn't make a sound as he jumped up and down with joy.

Arty wasted no time when he got up the next morning.

He grabbed his sketchbook and went straight to his easel. Brushes in hand, he started painting a picture that would represent the day he and his mom spent together picnicking in the wheat field. Once the painting dried, he wrapped it and hid it away.

Saturday afternoon came soon enough and Arty pretended to be surprised when all his art was on display out in the front yard. Everyone who was a part of his project was there, including lots of classmates and even his teacher. Arty didn't know if he would ever become famous, but that day he certainly felt that way.

Once all the food was gone and the celebrating slowed, Arty announced that he would be giving all his art away to everyone who had helped him with his project. Somehow, his mother was left out and seemed a bit sad about not receiving a painting.

Arty let his mom think she wasn't getting anything for a few minutes before he ran off and pulled the wrapped painting out from behind a tree. As she unwrapped his artwork tears rolled down her face. She turned to Arty and told him, "You'll always be my master painter."

Made in the USA
Monee, IL
23 December 2020